No Time for Christmas

No Time for Christmas

by **Judy Delton**
illustrations by **Anastasia Mitchell**

Carolrhoda Books, Inc./Minneapolis

This book is available in two editions:
Library binding by Carolrhoda Books, Inc.
Soft cover by First Avenue Editions
241 First Avenue North
Minneapolis, Minnesota 55401

For Jennifer

Library of Congress Cataloging-in-Publication Data

Delton, Judy.
    No time for Christmas.

    (Carolrhoda on my own books)
    Summary: While planning to give surprise Christmas
gifts to each other, Bear and Brimhall come to a
realization about the meaning of Christmas.
    [1. Christmas—Fiction. 2. Friendship—Fiction.
3. Bears—Fiction] I. Mitchell, Anastasia, ill.
II. Title. III. Series: Carolrhoda on my own book.
PZ7.D388No   1988   [E]   88-1020
ISBN 0-87614-327-3 (lib. bdg.)
ISBN 0-87616-503-9 (pbk.)

Manufactured in the United States of America

2   3   4   5   6   7   8   9   10   98   97   96   95   94   93   92   91   90   89

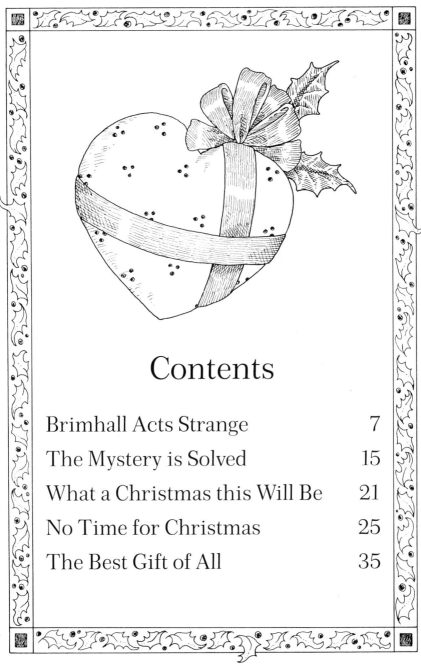

Contents

BRIMHALL
ACTS STRANGE

It was three weeks before Christmas.
Bear and Brimhall were just
sitting down to dinner.
"Coffee, tea, or milk?"
asked Brimhall.

Bear looked up in surprise.
"Why...er...milk would be fine,"
he said.
Brimhall poured milk
into Bear's glass.
"And will there be anything else?"
he asked.
"Brimhall, everything is right here
on the table," said Bear.
Brimhall lit the candle.
He turned the radio on
and soft music played.
The cousins helped themselves
to Bear's stew.

Suddenly Brimhall stood up.

He picked up his own plate.

Then he picked up Bear's plate.

Then he picked up the dish of stew.

He lined up all the dishes

on his left arm.

Brimhall bowed to Bear
and carried the dishes
to the kitchen.
"Brimhall, I wasn't finished yet!"

Brimhall came back from the kitchen
with two dishes of ice cream.
He set one in front of Bear
and one at his own place.
"Chocolate, raspberry, or
butterscotch sauce?" he asked.
"We don't *have* chocolate, raspberry,
or butterscotch sauce!" said Bear.
"What has gotten into you?"
"Why...er...nothing, Bear,"
said Brimhall.
"Nothing at all."
He ate his ice cream quickly
and blew out the candle.

"Well," Brimhall said
as he pushed back his chair,
"I'm going out for a while."
Bear looked up from his ice cream.
"Where are you going?" he asked.
"It seems like you've been gone
every evening lately."
But Brimhall was already out the door.

THE MYSTERY
IS SOLVED

There was a knock on the door.

Bear answered it.

"Why, Roger, how fine it is

to see you.

Come in."

"I thought I would come by
and play a game of chess with you
since Brimhall has been
working nights," said Roger.
"Working?" said Bear.
"What do you mean, working?"
"Why, Brimhall is a waiter now,
you know," said Roger.
"Brimhall? A *waiter*?"
"Didn't he tell you?" asked Roger.
"He is working at *The Foodery*
until he has enough money to buy
a special Christmas present for you."
"A special Christmas present?"
said Bear.

"Oh, dear!" Roger covered his mouth.
"Maybe I was not supposed
to say anything."

Bear frowned as he
got out the chess board.
He frowned through two games of chess.
He was still frowning when Roger left.

"I would like to get Brimhall
a special present for Christmas too,"
Bear said to himself
as he locked the door.
"But I don't have any money,"
he mumbled as he got ready for bed.
Suddenly Bear snapped his claws.
"Why didn't I think of that before?"

Bear wrote a note for Brimhall
to find in the morning.
Then he went to bed.
He fell asleep
with a smile on his face.

WHAT A CHRISTMAS
THIS WILL BE!

When Brimhall got out of bed
the next afternoon,
he found the note.
"I will be home at six o'clock.
Love, Bear," he read.

Brimhall sighed.

"But that is when I leave for work.

I guess I will have to

eat supper alone tonight."

At three o'clock the phone rang.

"Brimhall? This is Roger!"

He sounded out of breath.

"I was just at *Burro's Boutique*

and guess who waited on me?

BEAR!"

"Bear?" said Brimhall.

"Why would Bear wait on you?"

"He is working there," said Roger.

"He wants to earn enough money to buy

a special Christmas present for you."

"Oh, my!" said Brimhall

as he hung up the phone.

"What a Christmas this will be!
Bear will be surprised to see
a special present for him too!
Why, this will be
our best Christmas ever!"

NO TIME FOR CHRISTMAS

Every morning Bear hurried off
to *Burro's Boutique.*
Every evening by the time he got home,
Brimhall was at work as a waiter.
The cousins hardly saw each other.
They each planned the fine gifts
they would buy.

"I think Bear would like that
speedy-cook oven in Greenwood's
store window," said Brimhall to himself
on the way to work.
"Why, he could cook his honey-nut cake
in half the time."
Brimhall pictured the oven
under the Christmas tree
on Christmas morning,
with a big red bow around it.
"I simply have to earn enough money
to buy it," he said.
As Brimhall passed *Burro's Boutique*,
he saw Bear waiting on his
last customer of the day.
"I hope you like your new red sandals,"
he was saying to Sparrow.

Brimhall noticed that
Bear looked tired.
Brimhall hurried on to work.

Bear locked the door of the shop
and started home.
It was snowing, and the village trees
were decorated with colored lights.
Bear began to hum a Christmas carol.
He felt warm all over,
thinking about the fine gift he
would buy for Brimhall.

"I think Brimhall would like that fiddle
in the window of the music store,"
he said to himself.
He pictured the fiddle
under the Christmas tree
on Christmas morning,
with a red bow around it.
"I must earn enough money to buy it."

Bear took the path past *The Foodery*.
Brimhall was inside
waiting on a customer.
"Tonight I am hungry for spaghetti
with tomato sauce," said Frog.
Brimhall shook his head.
"Try the Bearnaise sauce," he said.
"It is much better."
Brimhall started for the kitchen.

Bear noticed that Brimhall
was walking slower than usual.

Bear went home and opened
a can of beans for his dinner.
They did not taste good to him.
"It is lonely eating by myself,"
said Bear.

The next morning on the way to work,
Bear noticed that every house
on the lane was decorated except his.
And every house but his had a
Christmas tree in the window.
"We do not even have a wreath
on our door," said Bear.
"I have not had time to make one.
And I have not talked to Brimhall
for over a week," he said.

As Bear walked into the boutique,
a tear rolled down his cheek.

THE BEST
GIFT OF ALL

One evening on the way to work,
Brimhall passed Roger's house.
"Brimhall," called Roger.
"Come in and have a Christmas cookie."

Brimhall had forgotten
about Christmas cookies.
Every other year,
Bear had baked Christmas cookies
with red and green sugar on them.
"Thank you," said Brimhall.
"I believe I will."

Red bells hung in Roger's house.
In the living room was a tall tree
with a silver star on top.
Roger made a pot of tea and put
a plate of cookies on the table.
"You have your Christmas tree up early,"
said Brimhall.
"Early?" said Roger.
"Tomorrow is Christmas Eve, Brimhall!"
"Dear me," said Brimhall,
"I didn't realize that.
We do not even have a
Christmas tree yet."
Sadly, Brimhall ate a Christmas cookie.

"Today I am busy wrapping presents,"
Roger chattered.
"All of my relatives
are coming tomorrow.

We are going caroling together,
then we will have a big dinner
and open gifts.
Christmas is the time to be
with those you love, you know."
"I will be working at night,
and Bear will be working all day,"
said Brimhall.
"It will not feel like Christmas at all."
"Dear me," said Roger,
trying to think of a way
to cheer Brimhall.
"But you will be able
to buy each other fine gifts."
"What good are fine gifts
if we never see each other?"
said Brimhall,
putting on his hat to leave.

Brimhall kicked snow
all the way to work.
He looked at the decorations
and lights on the houses.
He listened to sleigh bells
jingling past him.
He tasted the crumbs of Roger's

Christmas cookies in his mouth.

"It will not be Christmas at our house,"
said Brimhall to a snowdrift.
"We do not have a tree,
we have no decorations,
and there is no Bear."

When Brimhall got home from work,
he did not sleep well.
He got up early in the morning
to talk to Bear
before Bear went to work.
"Why, Brimhall, you look tired.
What are you doing up so early?"
Bear asked.
"I wanted to buy you a new
speedy-cook oven for Christmas,
so you could bake your
honey-nut cakes in half the time."
"But I have no time
to bake anymore, Brimhall,"
said Bear sadly.

"I am working because I want
to buy you the fiddle
in the music store window."
"And I have no time
to play the fiddle, Bear.
But I think I know what we *can* give
each other for Christmas."
"What is that, Brimhall?"
"Christmas Eve."
"But we are working," said Bear.
"I think we need to be together at
Christmas more than we need presents."
Bear looked at Brimhall.

"Then we can bake cookies,"
he said, "and cook Christmas dinner!"
"And trim the tree and make wreaths!"
added Brimhall.

"Squirrel and Chipmunk
are looking for jobs," said Bear.
"We can give them ours," said Brimhall.
"For Christmas!"

Brimhall put his arm around his cousin.
Together they looked out the window
and watched the snow fall.
Bear began to sing.